Neil Gaiman

THE DANGEROUS ALPHABET

Illustrated by

Gris Grimly

HarperCollinsPublishers

The Dangerous Alphabet
Text copyright © 2008 by Neil Gaiman Illustrations copyright © 2008 by Gris Grimly

Manufactured in China. All rights reserved. No part of this book may be used or reproduced in any manner whatsoever without written permission except
in the case of brief quotations embodied in critical articles and reviews. For information address HarperCollins Children's Books, a division of HarperCollins Publishers,
1350 Avenue of the Americas, New York, NY 10019. www.harpercollinschildrens.com

Library of Congress Cataloging-in-Publication Data is available.
ISBN 978-0-06-078333-4 (trade bdg.) — ISBN 978-0-06- 078334-1 (lib. bdg.)

Title and initials hand lettered by Gris Grimly. Design by Dana Fritts.
1 2 3 4 5 6 7 8 9 10 ❖ First Edition

A piratical ghost story in thirteen ingenious but potentially disturbing rhyming couplets, originally conceived as a confection both to amuse and to entertain by Mr. Neil Gaiman, scrivener, and then doodled, elaborated upon, illustrated, and beaten soundly by Mr. Gris Grimly, etcher and illuminator, featuring two brave children, their diminutive but no less courageous gazelle, and a large number of extremely dangerous trolls, monsters, bugbears, creatures, and other such nastinesses, many of which have perfectly disgusting eating habits and ought not, under any circumstances, to be encouraged.

Please Note: The alphabet, as given in this publication, is *not to be relied upon* and has a dangerous flaw that an eagle-eyed reader may be able to discern.

A is for Always,
that's where we embark;

B is for Boat, pushing off in the dark;

is the way
that we find and we look;

D is for
DIAMONDS,
the bait on the hook;

E's
for the Evil
that lures and
entices;

F is for Fear

and its many devices;

G is for Good,
as in hero,
and Morning;

H is for "Help Me!"
—a cry,
and a warning;

I am the author
who scratches
these rhymes;

J is the joke monsters make of their crimes;

is, like 'eaven, their last destination;

M is for Mirrors
you'll stare in
forever;

N is for Night, and for Nothing, and Never;

O is for OveNS, far under the street;

is for Piracy, blunt or discreet;

is for Quiet
(bar one muffled scream);

R

is a River that flows like a dream;

is for—somewhere—a Skull and its Smile;

T is for Treasure
heaped into a pile;

are
the reader
who
shivers
with dread;

W's **Warnings** went over your head;

V is for
Vile deeds
done in the
Night;

marked the spot, if we read the map right;

(**Z** waits alone, and it's not for a thing).

JP   Gaiman, Neil.

            The dangerous
            alphabet.

DATE			